the BAD GUYS

in

MISSION
UNPLUCKABLE

TEXT AND ILLUSTRATIONS COPYRIGHT © 2015 BY AARON BLABEY

ALL RIGHTS RESERVED. PUBLISHED BY SCHOLASTIC INC., *PUBLISHERS SINCE 1920*, 557 BROADWAY, NEW YORK, NY 10012. SCHOLASTIC AND ASSOCIATED LOGOS ARE TRADEMARKS AND/OR REGISTERED TRADEMARKS OF SCHOLASTIC INC. THIS EDITION PUBLISHED UNDER LICENSE FROM SCHOLASTIC AUSTRALIA PTY LIMITED. FIRST PUBLISHED BY SCHOLASTIC AUSTRALIA PTY LIMITED IN 2015.

THE PUBLISHER DOES NOT HAVE ANY CONTROL OVER AND DOES NOT ASSUME ANY RESPONSIBILITY FOR AUTHOR OR THIRD-PARTY WEBSITES OR THEIR CONTENT.

NO PART OF THIS PUBLICATION MAY BE REPRODUCED, STORED IN A RETRIEVAL SYSTEM, OR TRANSMITTED IN ANY FORM OR BY ANY MEANS, ELECTRONIC, MECHANICAL, PHOTOCOPYING, RECORDING, OR OTHERWISE, WITHOUT WRITTEN PERMISSION OF THE PUBLISHER. FOR INFORMATION REGARDING PERMISSION, WRITE TO SCHOLASTIC AUSTRALIA, AN IMPRINT OF SCHOLASTIC AUSTRALIA PTY LIMITED, 345 PACIFIC HIGHWAY, LINDFIELD NSW 2070 AUSTRALIA.

THIS BOOK IS A WORK OF FICTION. NAMES, CHARACTERS, PLACES, AND INCIDENTS ARE EITHER THE PRODUCT OF THE AUTHOR'S IMAGINATION OR ARE USED FICTITIOUSLY, AND ANY RESEMBLANCE TO ACTUAL PERSONS, LIVING OR DEAD, BUSINESS ESTABLISHMENTS, EVENTS, OR LOCALES IS ENTIRELY COINCIDENTAL.

LIBRARY OF CONGRESS CATALOGING-IN-PUBLICATION DATA

NAMES: BLABEY, AARON, AUTHOR.
TITLE: THE BAD GUYS IN MISSION UNPLUCKABLE / AARON BLABEY.
OTHER TITLES: MISSION UNPLUCKABLE
DESCRIPTION: NEW YORK : SCHOLASTIC INC., 2017. | SERIES: THE BAD GUYS ; 2 | SUMMARY: STILL YEARNING TO BE SEEN AS HEROES, WOLF, SHARK, SNAKE, AND PIRANHA SET OUT TO RESCUE TEN THOUSAND CHICKENS FROM A HIGH-TECH CAGE FARM—BUT ONE UNEXPECTED PROBLEM IS MR. SNAKE HIMSELF, ALSO KNOWN AS "THE CHICKEN SWALLOWER."
IDENTIFIERS: LCCN 2016013788 | ISBN 9780545912419
SUBJECTS: LCSH: ANIMALS—JUVENILE FICTION. | RESCUES—JUVENILE FICTION. | CHICKENS—JUVENILE FICTION. | HEROES—JUVENILE FICTION. | CYAC: ANIMALS—FICTION. | RESCUES—FICTION. | CHICKENS—FICTION. | HEROES—FICTION. | HUMOROUS STORIES. | GSAFD: HUMOROUS FICTION.
CLASSIFICATION: LCC PZ7.B52864 BE 2016 (PRINT) | DDC [FIC]   DC23
LC RECORD AVAILABLE AT HTTPS://LCCN.LOC.GOV/2016013788

ISBN 978-0-545-91241-9

15 14 13 12 11   18 19 20 21

PRINTED IN THE U.S.A.   23
FIRST U.S. PRINTING 2017

· AARON BLABEY ·

the BAD GUYS

SCHOLASTIC INC.

in

MISSION UNPLUCKABLE

NEWS FLASH!

PANIC AT THE DOG POUND!

We interrupt this program to bring you a breaking news story.

TIFFANY FLUFFIT is our reporter on the scene. Tiffany, what can you tell us?

CHUCK MELON

Thanks, Chuck!

Well, there have been **SHOCKING** scenes at the **DOG POUND** today.

It seems some kind of **CRAZED GANG** burst in, smashed down a wall, and then drove away in a very loud hot-rod car, causing **200 TERRIFIED PUPPY DOGS** to run away in fright.

TIFFANY FLUFFIT 6 NEWS

I have with me **MR. GRAHAM PLONKER**, Chief of Dog Pound Security.

Mr. Plonker, how would you describe these **MONSTERS?**

Uh . . . well . . . it all happened so fast, but . . . I'm pretty sure there were four of them . . .

I mean, there was definitely a **WOLF**.

6 NEWS

EXCLUSIVE FOOTAGE!

A really *mean*-looking wolf, with pointy teeth.

And there was a **SNAKE**.

6 NEWS

HAVE YOU SEEN THIS SNAKE?

A very *ugly* snake, who also seemed very cranky for some reason . . .

Uh, then there was a **YOUNG LADY**...

PRETTY GIRL? OR DEADLY SHARK?

... or possibly a gigantic **SHARK**. It was hard to tell which ...

Oh yeah, and there was also some kind of nasty little fish.

MUTANT SARDINE ON THE LOOSE!

Maybe a **SARDINE**.

Not sure.

But, Mr. Plonker, would
   you say that these
   villains seemed . . .

DANGEROUS?

Oh yes, Tiffany. They're
dangerous, all right.

In fact, I'd say we are dealing
with some *serious* . . .

· CHAPTER 1 ·
OK, LET'S TRY THAT AGAIN

See, Wolf? No one is **EVER** going to believe we're good guys. I'm getting out of here before the cops come looking for us.

Oh, **NO** you don't, Mr. Snake! We're not going to quit now. We're just getting started.

Don't forget **HOW GOOD** it felt to
rescue those dogs!

All we need to do now is make sure that
everyone can **SEE** that we're **HEROES**.

We just need to do something
SO AWESOME that the whole
world will sit up and take notice!

What did you have in
mind, Mr. Wolf?

You want us to break
into a chicken farm?

Chickens?

Did you say
... *chickens*?

A chicken farm?
But that little chickie
looks happy. She doesn't
need to be rescued . . .

Oh, really?

Well, take a look INSIDE
Sunnyside Chicken Farm, fellas.

10,000 CHICKENS!

Stuffed into **TINY** cages!

24 hours a day!

With **NO** sunlight!

And **NO** room to run and play!

But that's awful!
That's the worst thing
I've ever heard!

What are we waiting for?!

WE NEED TO SET THOSE
LITTLE CHICKIE-BABIES
FREE!

Let's go! Let's go! Let's go!
Let's go! Let's go! Let's go!
Let's go! Let's go! Let's go!
Let's go! Let's go! Let's go!

LET'S GO!

What's up with
Mr. Snake?

I don't know. I guess he
just really loves chickens.

DROOL!

DROOL!

Oh yeah . . . sorry.
I was just thinking that chickens are
delicious—I mean, *DELIGHTFUL*—
and I think we need to save them all
RIGHT NOW.

Oh, if only it were that
simple, my friend.
But I'm afraid I have
some bad news . . .

It's a **MAXIMUM SECURITY CHICKEN FARM** with **STEEL WALLS** that are thirty feet high and eight feet thick!

There are **NO WINDOWS** and all the doors are **HEAVILY GUARDED.**

SUNNYSIDE
INC.

And even if you *did* get inside, you'd be caught instantly because . . .

If you touch the FLOOR, an **ALARM** goes off!

If you touch the WALLS, an **ALARM** goes off!

And if you walk into the LASER BEAMS, an **ALARM** goes off!

• FLOOR ALARMS

• WALL ALARMS

• LASER BEAM ALARMS

Did you say
LASER BEAMS?
Why are you even showing us
this, *chico*? We don't have the
skills to pull off a job like this!

No, we don't.
But I know a guy who does.

Who?

· CHAPTER 2 ·
the
FREAKY GEEK

Hey, dudes! It's totally
awesome to meet you!

Aieeeeee!

RUN, *CHICOS*! It's a

TARANTULA!!!

I'm sorry about this, Legs.
I don't know what's
wrong with them.

Aw, it's cool.
Happens all the time.

LEGS?!

You *know* this monster?!

What were you thinking,
bringing a tarantula into
our clubhouse?

Can't breathe . . .
spider . . .
Mommy . . .
Mommy . . .
I want my mommy . . .

Mr. Shark! Pull yourself together!
You guys should be ASHAMED of yourselves!
LEGS is just like us.
He's a GOOD GUY with a BAD reputation.

Aw, thanks,
Wolfie.

He's **DANGEROUS,** man.

Yeah!
And why isn't he
wearing any pants?

But **NOBODY** can access that! There's no way you can hack into their system. That's the toughest security there is!

Yeah, it *is* kind of tricky.

TAP! TAP! TAP! TAP! TAP! TAP! TAP! TAP!

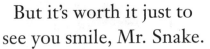

But it's worth it just to see you smile, Mr. Snake.

Not for a **SUPERHACKER** like Legs!
He's a computer **GENIUS**. And he has a plan
that will get us inside that chicken farm.

Thanks, Wolfie. But first,
I'd better put this back
the way I found it. We are
good guys, after all . . .

ACC
Nam
Status
Action:

. . . and I wouldn't like
to get us in trouble.
Sorry, Mr. Snake.
You're *dangerous* again,
I'm afraid.

DANGER
DO NOT
APPROA

Hey!

This is **SO** cool, guys! I'm so happy to be part of the team. And I bet by this time tomorrow, we're totally going to be **BESTIES!**

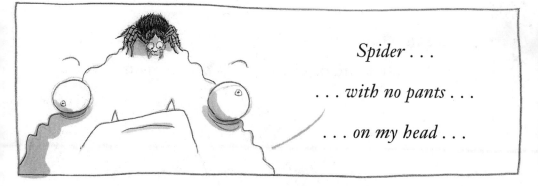

Spider . . .

. . . with no pants . . .

. . . on my head . . .

PAINT!

Hey, *chico.* I got one word for you— *pants.*

SPLAT!

· CHAPTER 3 ·

MISSION, LIKE, TOTALLY IMPOSSIBLE

OK, dudes, I took your advice and found
myself some clothes. What do you think?

I can still see his

BIG FURRY BUTT.

Cut it out,
Piranha.
Just listen
to him.

OK.

To get you guys inside
Sunnyside Chicken Farm,
all I need to do is hack into
their main computer and
switch off all the alarms.

BUT

there's a problem . . .

The security is
SO HIGH
that I can't do it from here.

I need you guys to plug
THIS THING
into their computer,
so I can access it.

Once you do that, I can
SHUT IT ALL DOWN
and get you to those
chickens.

Wait a minute. You're telling
us that you can hack into my
police file, but you **CAN'T**
get into a CHICKEN FARM
without our help?

Yeah. It's WEIRD.
This is one SCARY
chicken farm, dude.

But if it's so scary, how do we
get to the computer?
Wolf said there's no way into
the building!

Well, there is **ONE** way.

But it sure isn't easy . . .

There's a
SMALL HATCH
on the roof.

You'll need to go
through the hatch
and **DROP**
150 feet on a rope
to the computer
below. Once you
get to it, **JUST
PLUG ME IN**.

BUT!

If you touch the
WALLS or the
FLOOR, the
ALARMS will
go off and you'll
get caught.

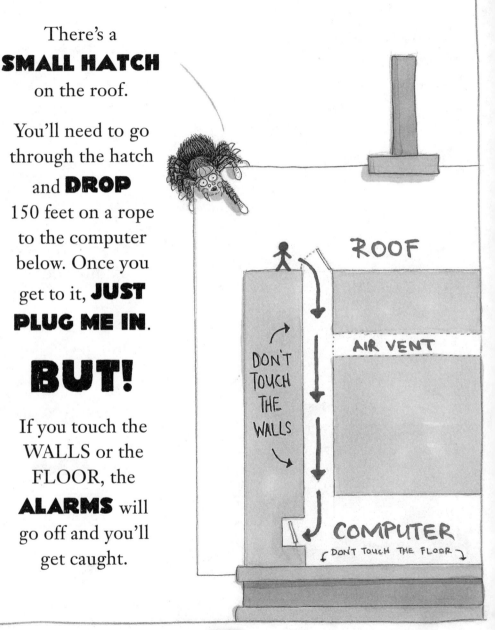

ROOF

DON'T
TOUCH
THE
WALLS

AIR VENT

COMPUTER

DON'T TOUCH THE FLOOR

That's it?
That doesn't sound so bad.

I'm not finished.

Once you plug me in, you have to climb back up the rope, crawl through this **AIR VENT**, and follow the tunnel to the CHICKEN CAGES.

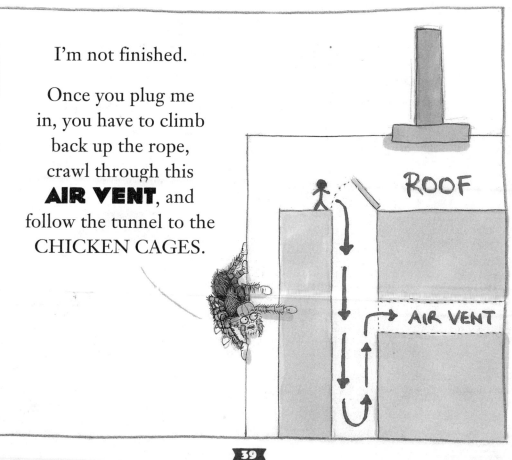

ROOF

AIR VENT

Like I said, that doesn't sound so bad.

I'M STILL NOT FINISHED.
You see, before you reach the chicken cages,
you'll come to the **LASER BEAMS**.
And if you touch one, the alarms will go off.

Oh, and they'll zap you.
And they *really* hurt.

LASERS

→ AIR VENT →

But why are the lasers still on?
I thought you were going to shut
down all the alarms.

I will.
The **OTHER** alarms will be off.

But the **LASER ALARMS**
can only be turned off by hand.
You have to flick a switch
once you're inside.

So . . . we just switch them off?

Yep.

That *still* doesn't sound so bad.

That's because I'm **STILL NOT FINISHED!**

The switch is on the OTHER SIDE of the laser beams, so you have to GO **THROUGH** THEM to reach it!

CHICKENS
THIS WAY

You finished yet?

Uhhh . . . yep.

Good! Because
that sounds

LOCO!

There's **NO WAY** we
can pull this off, man!

Oh yes, we can!

But **ONLY** if we work as a **TEAM!**

So, Snake and Piranha—

you guys are coming with ME!

We are going to **GET INSIDE**,

plug **THIS THING** into the computer, and

GET TO THOSE CHICKENS!

This is going to be

GREAT!

But . . . what about me?

You're going to be working with me, Big Guy.
It's OUR JOB to get these guys in and out of there safely!
Isn't this awesome? You and I are going to SPEND A
LOT OF TIME TOGETHER!

*Oh . . . that's . . .
great . . . but . . .
I think . . .
I'm going . . .
to cry . . .*

No time for tears, Mr. Shark.

WE'VE GOT CHICKENS TO SAVE!

· CHAPTER 4 ·
DOWN THE HATCH

Hey, what are you guys
doing all the way over there?

Hey, Tarantula! What's with the stupid suits?

Shhh! Not so loud, Mr. Piranha. These suits are GREAT! They'll keep you cool and make you really hard to spot.

Each suit has a microphone and earpiece, so we can all talk to each other.

Hey, Wolf, do you really promise there'll be chickens down there?

It's a **CHICKEN** FARM! Of course there'll be chickens. Why are you so worried about that?

Oh, no reason.

I just really **LOVE** chickens, man.

They're so nice to eat— I mean, they're so nice to *MEET*.

Yeah . . .

OK. Mr. Shark? You know what to do . . .

Gently lower us on the count of three.

ONE . . .
TWO . . .

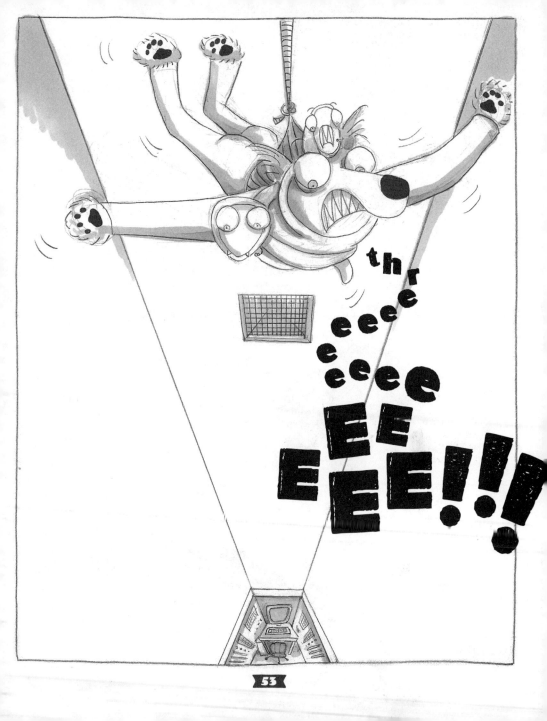

OK. OK. OK. Well, the walls are a *little* closer than I expected.

Mr. Shark! Whatever you do, make sure you lower us *SLOWLY*.

I hear you.

Do you need a hand, big buddy?

BOING!

EEEEEEEEEE

FOOF!

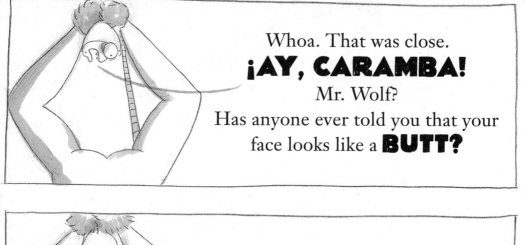

Whoa. That was close.
¡AY, CARAMBA!
Mr. Wolf?
Has anyone ever told you that your
face looks like a **BUTT?**

What?

Oh. Sorry. My mistake.

Hey, look! The computer!
I think I can reach it . . .

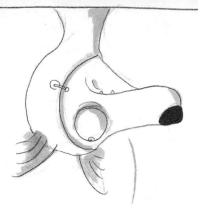

He didn't see us.
Why didn't he see us?

Shhh! I don't know.
He must have really bad eyesight.
Um . . . OK . . .
Any suggestions on what we do now?

Are you kidding?
WE GET
OUT OF
HERE!
SHARK?!
ABORT!
ABORT!
PULL US
UP NOW!

Piranha? You're not going to do anything crazy, are you?

"Crazy" is what I bring to the party, *chico*. Wish me luck . . .

BOING!

Piranha! No!

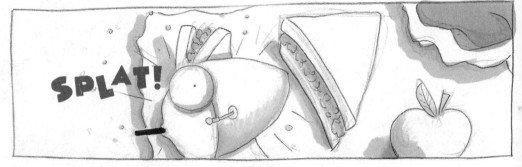

SPLAT!

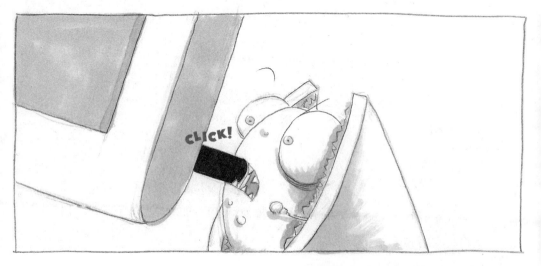

The alarms are off! I repeat—the ALARMS ARE OFF! You are safe to enter the AIR VENT.

This was a one-way ticket, *chico*.

WHAT? We can't just leave you behind!

You have to, *hermanos*. There is no other way.

Go and save those little chickens, man. Save them for **ME!**

Wolf! Snap out of it!
SHARK! Pull us up!

You got it.

Hurry up, man.
Just get in the vent, will you?

Look at him
down there!

What a brave
little guy!

He sacrificed
himself for us.

*Adiós,
chicos.*

Yeah, yeah. Let's do this.
I'm starving—I mean,
I'm *STARTING* to want to
save some chickens. Yep.

You're
right.
We
should
go.

Adiós,
Mr. Piranha.

Stay safe.

Easy for you
to say, baby.

· CHAPTER 5 ·
MIND THE GAP

See, Mr. Snake?
This is what I've been talking about—without Mr. Piranha, we would **NEVER** have made it this far. **THAT'S** what being on a team is all about.

COOPERATION.

Yeah, yeah, yeah, that's *so* interesting, but WHERE ARE THE CHICKENS, man?

Just up ahead, I'd say.

This bit has been a lot easier than I thought. I really don't know what all the fuss was ab—

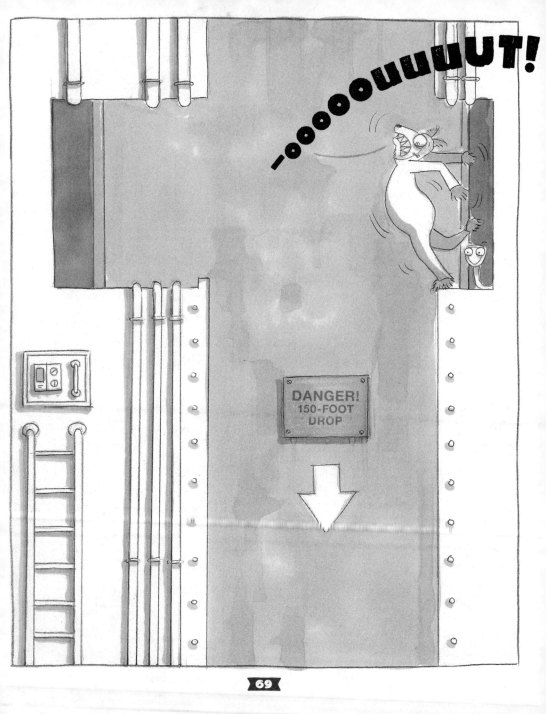

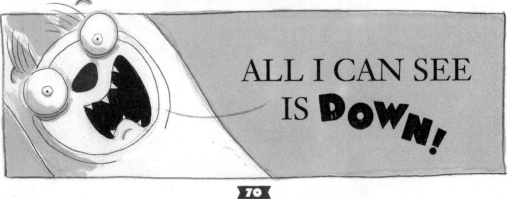

Hey! I have an idea.
Why don't you stay here?

I'll go and eat—
I mean, *GREET*
those chickens.

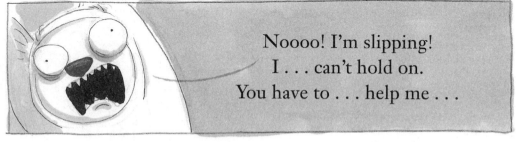

Noooo! I'm slipping!
I . . . can't hold on.
You have to . . . help me . . .

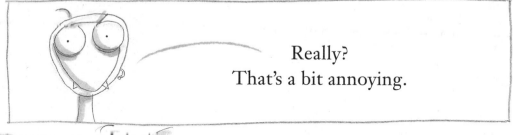

Really?
That's a bit annoying.

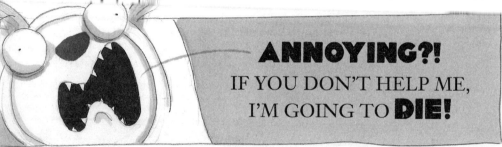

ANNOYING?!
IF YOU DON'T HELP ME,
I'M GOING TO **DIE!**

Wow. It's always **"ME, ME, ME"** with you, isn't it?

SLIP!

SLIP!

Oh no!

GRAB!

Hey!
Wait a second.
That's better!

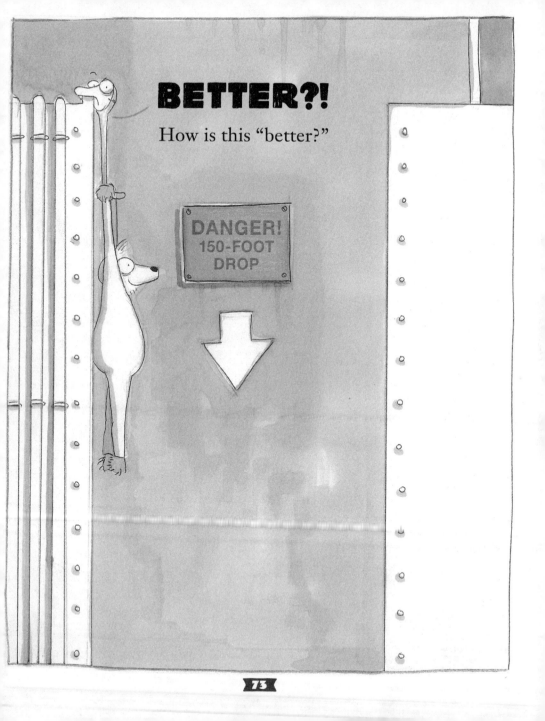

BETTER?!

How is this "better?"

DANGER!
150-FOOT
DROP

You need to go
on a diet, man.
You really do.

Now, let's think.

What do we do?

We're trapped.

It's not just ME
that's trapped. And
it's not just YOU.
It's **US**.

We're trapped as
a **TEAM**. So we
need to get out of
this as a **TEAM**.

I'VE **GOT** IT!

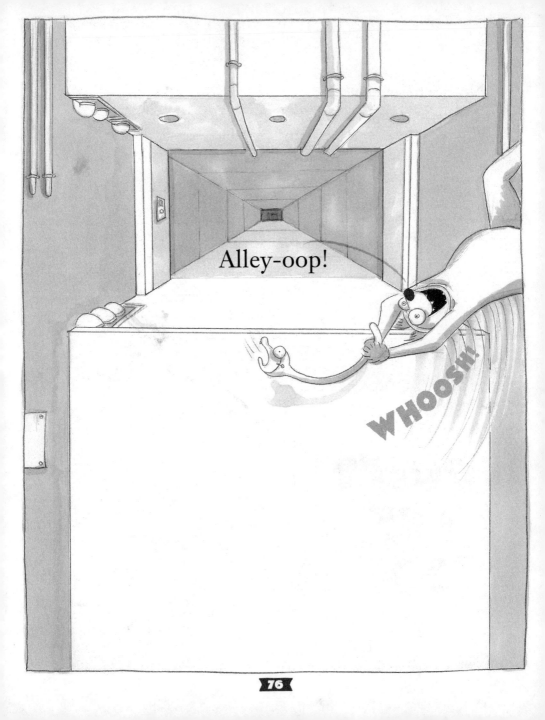

• CHAPTER 6 •
LET'S START OVER

That's not good.

Piranha?
Can you hear me?

Mr. Shark? Is that you?

I'm about to be a monkey's lunch here, man.

You sit tight, Mr. P. I'm coming to get you.

BOING!

Can I help, **BIG FELLA?**

ARRRRGGGGHHH!

PLEASE don't . . .
can't breathe . . .
please don't . . .
really please don't . . .
can't breathe . . .

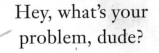

Hey, what's your problem, dude?

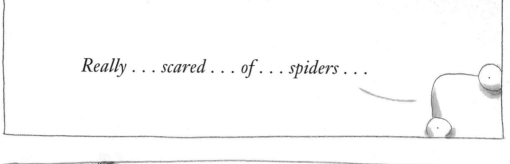

Really . . . scared . . . of . . . spiders . . .

Uh-huh. And why is that?
It's OK, you can tell me.

OK, well . . .
     you're **FREAKY** to look at because
you have **TOO MANY EYES** and
TOO MANY LEGS
and I'm **SO** creeped
out by you that
**I MIGHT
THROW UP!**

Well . . .

since I can't help being a tarantula in the same way

that you CAN'T HELP BEING A

MASSIVE, TERRIFYING SEA MONSTER,

I wonder
if you could just

GET OVER IT

and then

MAYBE

I could help you rescue
your friend!

Um . . . OK.

I'm so sorry.
That was
really uncool.

It's OK.
That's good
advice.

Well . . . um . . . how are we
going to rescue that piranha?

I've heard you're pretty good
at disguises. Is that right?

I have my moments.

OK, well, I'm REALLY good at making stuff. So why don't we work together?

OK.

But what kind of disguise is going to get me inside a chicken farm?

Why don't you pull the feathers out of those pillows there, Mr. Shark, and I'll tell you my idea

· CHAPTER 7 ·
TRUST ME, I'M A SNAKE

Oh no! Look at those laser beams! I'll **NEVER** get through!

I think we have a problem.

CAGE ➡️

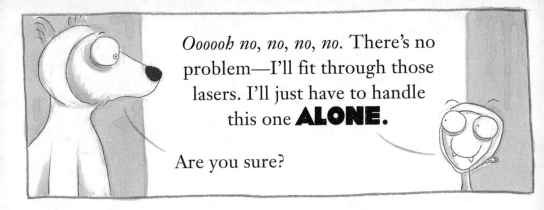

Oooooh no, no, no, no. There's no problem—I'll fit through those lasers. I'll just have to handle this one **ALONE.**

Are you sure?

Oh, ABSOLUTELY.
I'll just wriggle my way across and have a chicken feast—I mean . . . I'll get those chickens **RELEASED.**

Yeah.
Released.
Heh heh.

But you'll switch off the lasers when you get across?

Yeah, yeah, sure.

Just a little farther . . .

Ha!

YOU **MADE** IT!

You're amazing!

Now, just switch off the lasers so I can get across . . .

CAGES →

Hmmm, sure.

Just give me a few minutes to find the switch . . .

You take your time, little buddy!

YOU ROCK!

I'm just SO proud of these guys.

WHISTLE
WHISTLE

Geez, it's been fifteen minutes.

Are you OK over there, Mr. Snake?

Mr. Snake?

What are you doing over there?

In the dark?

Behind all those . . . **EMPTY** cages?

I TRUSTED YOU!
How could you do
something so awful?

I'm a SNAKE, man.
What did you expect?

NO, Mr. Snake.
YOU ARE A GOOD GUY.
And you're not leaving this building
without 10,000 healthy and happy
chickens—EVERY SINGLE
FLUFFY ONE OF THEM.
**ARE YOU
FEELING ME?**

· CHAPTER 8 ·
WHOLE LOTTA CHICKEN

¡Ay caramba!

This is the end, amigos!

Hey, Clive! One of the chickens escaped, but we've managed to catch it again.

What?

ARRGGHHH!!!

Yeah, I'm your **WORST** nightmare, *hombre*! I'm a piranha burger with **EXTRA SPICE!**

Mr. Shark?
Is that you?

Yep.

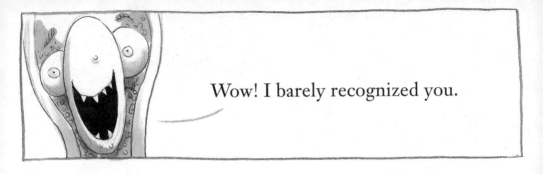

Wow! I barely recognized you.

Yeah, I know.
I'm good at disguises.

WHOOP! WHOOP! WHOOP!

OH NO! They've set off the alarm!

WHOOP! WHOOP! WHOOP!

But Wolf
and Snake
will be
trapped!

Guys! It's Legs!
Get out of there!
They're coming
for you!

WHOOP! WHOOP! WHOOP!

We're not leaving
without our *chicos*.

Or our
chickens.

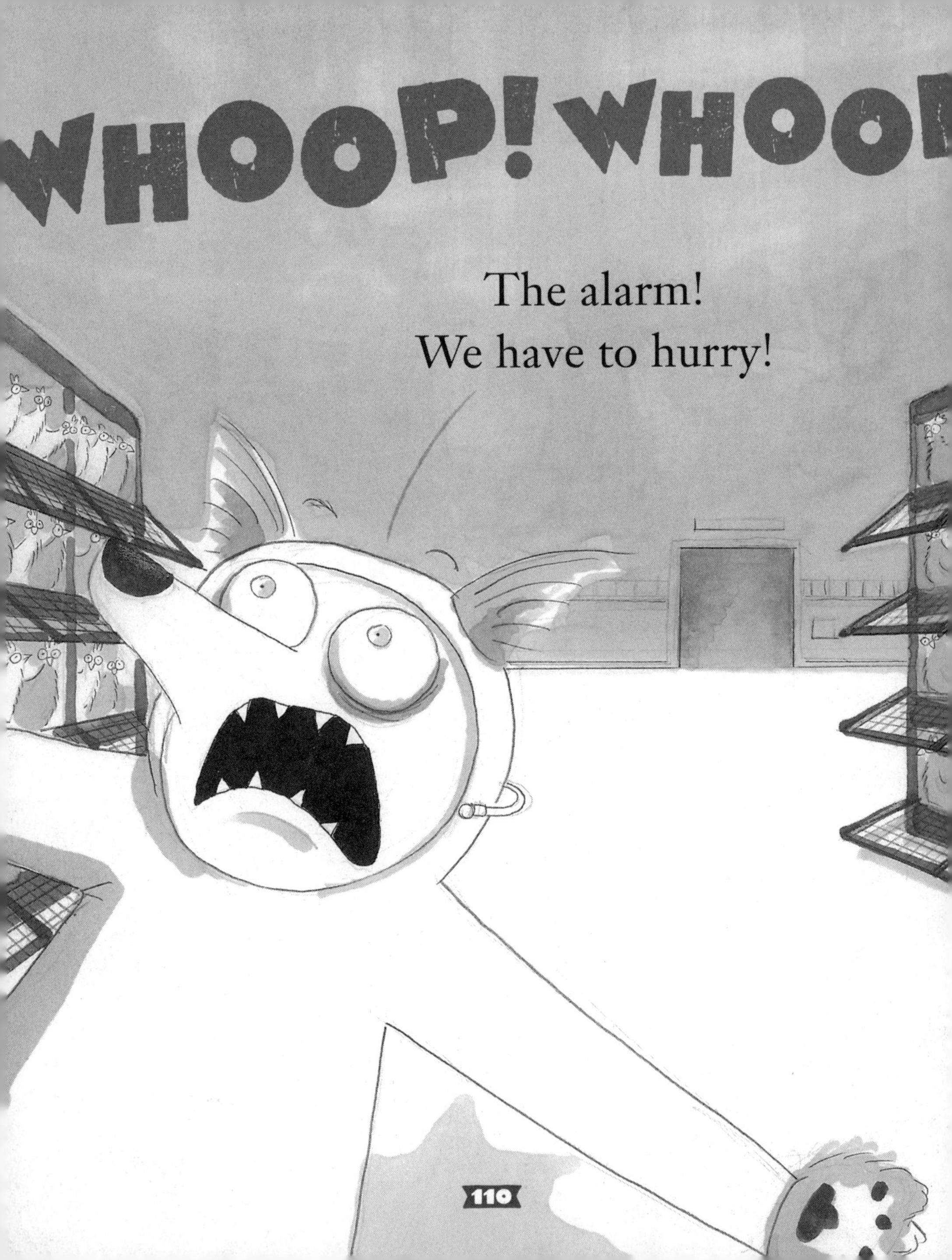
WHOOP! WHOO
The alarm!
We have to hurry!

We've opened the cages, but they won't run. What's wrong with these stupid chickens?

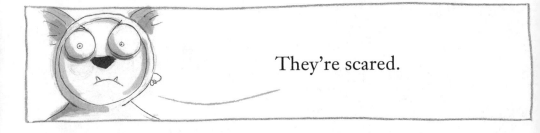

They're scared.

Of what?

OF THE CREEP WHO TRIED TO **EAT THEM!**

I couldn't help it.

I'm sorry.

Yeah, well, "sorry" won't help us now, Mr. Snake.

What are we going to do? The chickens are terrified.

They need someone to **FOLLOW**.

They need someone to **TRUST**.

They need . . .

Wow. That's one big chicken.

All right, girls. I know you're scared, but this is your **ONE CHANCE** to get out of this horrible place.

Do you understand?

THEN LET'S GET OUT OF HERE!

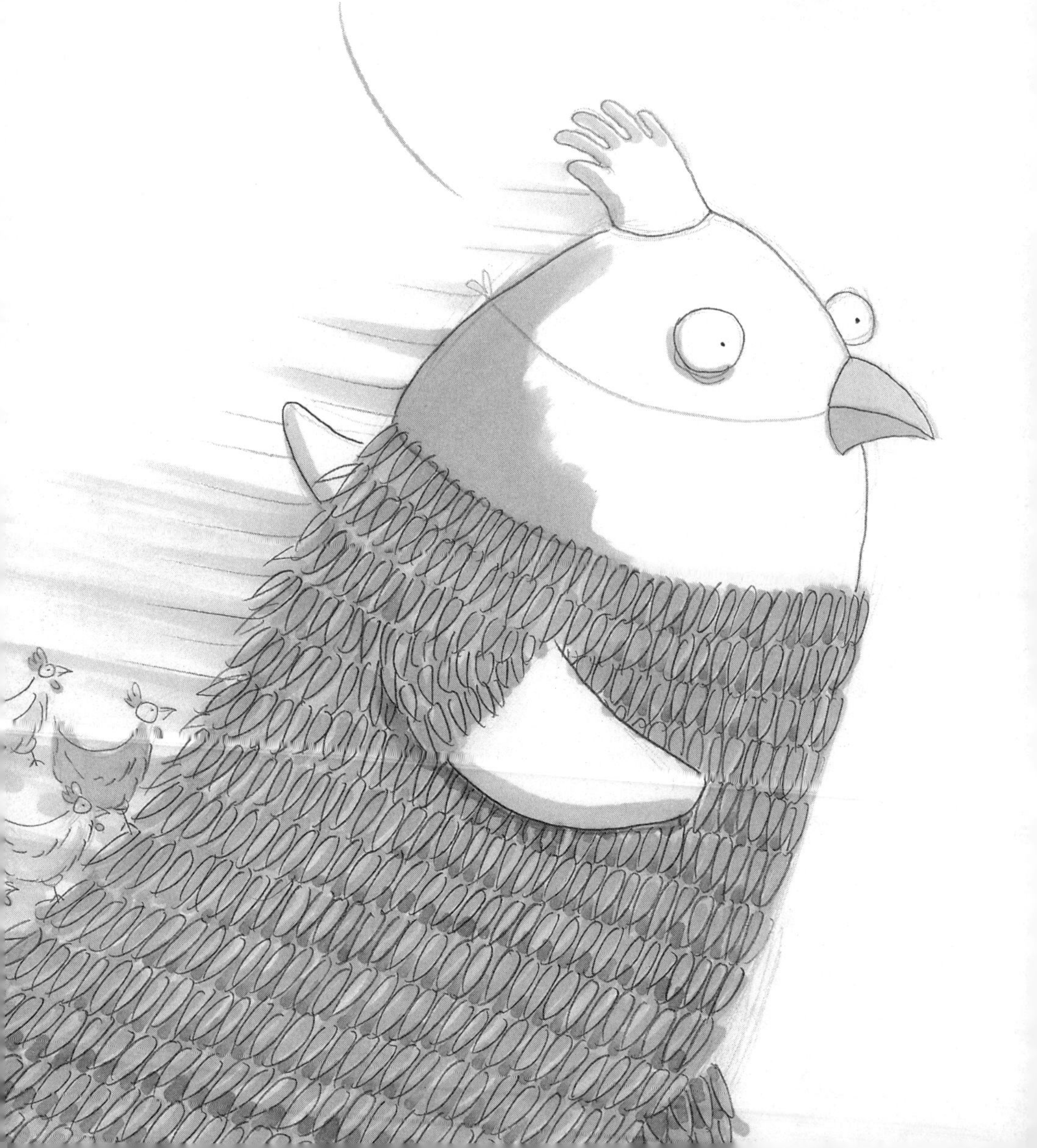

We're **TRAPPED!**

This is the **END!**

My chickens will
NEVER
be free!

Throw me at him!
It's your only chance!

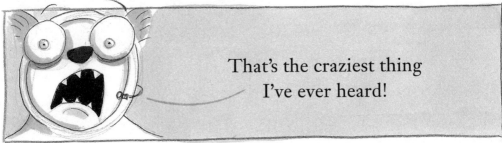

That's the craziest thing
I've ever heard!

This is my chance to do
some good, Mr. Wolf.

Hi. Let's play a game.
The first person to
open the door doesn't
get bitten by a snake.

You win.

· CHAPTER 9 ·
WHAT A TEAM

I am so proud of you guys!

10,000 chickens are free
because of **YOU!**

I think we're starting to get the hang of this hero thing, fellas.

And that means you, too, Mr. Snake.

OK, Huggy Bear. Let's not make a great big hairy deal out of it.

Aw, sure thing, you old grouch! Let's get out of here . . .

But . . .

What happened to the **CAR?!**

Oh yeah. While I was waiting for you guys to get back, I fitted it with **MONSTER TRUCK** tires and a **JET ENGINE**. I hope you don't mind?

We don't mind!

And I noticed that you seemed a little cramped in there, Mr. Shark, so I've modified your seat. If you don't like it, I can always put it back the way it was.

I . . . I *love* it, Legs.
You're very thoughtful.

Thank you.

Anytime, Mr. Shark.
Anytime at all.

I'm breathing.
It's all good.
I'm breathing.
It's all good.
I'm breathing.
It's all good.

SQUEAK!

Hey! Did
anybody else
hear that?

Hmmm.
It seems to be coming from that
CREEPY OLD HOUSE
next to the chicken farm that we . . .
somehow didn't notice. Perhaps it's
a chicken that's lost its way?

I didn't know chickens
could squeak . . .

Nope. My mistake.
There's nothing here. It's empty.

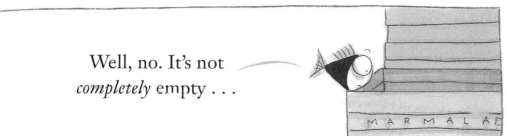

Well, no. It's not
completely empty . . .

MARMALA

Look!

GOOD GUYS?

And just because they call themselves
GOOD GUYS, they think they can

BREAK INTO MY CHICKEN FARM AND SET MY CHICKENS FREE?!

AND THEY THINK THEY CAN
GET AWAY WITH IT?

Well, we'll see about that. I shall make them pay.

Oh yes . . .

Boy, did these guys mess with the

WRONG

guinea pig!

See what happens when the Bad Guys get captured by a **REALLY bad guy**.

How will they escape from his evil lair? **Who** is that mysterious **NINJA** that seems to be following them? And **when** will they all stop trying to **EAT** each other?!

Don't miss their next **so-funny-you'll-wet-your-pants** adventure—

the **BAD GUYS** in
The Furball Strikes Back!

The Bad Guys are about to have a *really* BAD day . . .